# DETECTIVE VEX
## *Downfall*

**Frederik Dalgaard Kjaer**

Illustration: Istockphoto

Copyright © 2014 Frederik Dalgaard Kjaer

All rights reserved.

ISBN-13: 978-1500156336
ISBN-10: 1500156337

# DEDICATION

**THIS BOOK IS DEDICATED TO:**
My family and good friends who
have always been there for me.

Also, I want to credit my fantastic teachers
at Zürich International School (ZIS).

Christina Brodersen at ZIS for guiding me and
inspiring me onto the journey of writing books.

**A SPECIAL THANKS TO:**
My Mom & Dad
Yannick

# ACKNOWLEDGMENTS

### WHY I CHOSE TO WRITE THIS AWESOME DETECTIVE STORY:

I chose to write a book about the incredible Detective Vex because I love to read scary and thrilling books and stories myself. My favorite author and a big source of inspiration for me into the universe of science fiction is Derek Landy.

Also, I love writing and it was a great challenge for me to write a second book in English as I only started learning English 3.5 years ago. That was when I started in ZIS in grade 3.

And trust me, you will see more to Detective Vex.

# CONTENTS

Chapter 1:   In the Darkness ................................... 08
Chapter 2:   Rescued ............................................. 10
Chapter 3:   The Evil Master-Mind ......................... 12
Chapter 4:   On Recruit Search ............................... 14
Chapter 5:   The New Recruit ................................. 16
Chapter 6:   At the Hospital ................................... 18
Chapter 7:   Looking for Mary ................................ 20
Chapter 8:   Neferin Crox ....................................... 23
Chapter 9:   Preparing the Plan .............................. 26
Chapter 10:  The Plan is in Action .......................... 28
Chapter 11:  Scuba Diving ...................................... 32
Chapter 12:  Pirates ................................................ 35
Chapter 13:  One Makes it, Another Doesn't .......... 38
Chapter 14:  New Skill ............................................ 41
Chapter 15:  A Great Battle .................................... 42
Chapter 16:  Tides have Turned .............................. 44
Chapter 17:  Desmond ............................................ 47
Chapter 18:  Jonathan Johnson ............................... 49
Chapter 19:  Old Friend .......................................... 52
Chapter 20:  Saved .................................................. 55
Chapter 21:  Last Chapter ....................................... 58

# PROLOGUE

"Are you ready to poison Charlie?" Thiago Fernando Rodriguez asked.

"I sure am." Charlie answered.

They were sailing on a small boat in the middle of the big, blue Pacific Ocean. The two hardened criminals were just about to jump into the water with the little bottle of poison as a dagger flew right passed Thiago and caught Charlie in his throat. Charlie's body stumbled off the boat. Thiago turned around and saw an even smaller boat than his own and with the great detective Vex sailing it at extremely high speed.

"What are you doing here?" Thiago questioned.

"I'm here to make sure you don't do anything stupid, Mr. Thiago Fernando Rodriguez." Vex answered.

"What!? –To make sure I don't do anything stupid? And yet you're the one who travelled all the way out here not knowing that I have a thing that can kill you very, very easily."

"Oh yeah, and what might that be?" Vex asked, his fists turning into stone.

Thiago smiled grimly and suddenly vanished in the thin air as if evaporated through magic. Only, he then was suddenly standing on Vex's boat with a little dark container with a Hello Kitty sticker on it in his right hand.

"Oh hell … " Vex muttered as he flung himself off the boat.

Thiago threw the Japanese Engine bomb at Vex and then he vanished once again and just as the explosion completely destroyed Vex's small boat with a deafening blast.

# CHAPTER 1
# IN THE DARKNESS

Darkness … that was all Vex remembered. There had been darkness when Vex sunk into the cold Pacific Ocean. There had been darkness when he had landed in the uncomfortable water. Everything was just pure darkness. Then, a high pitched noise came into hearing range and seconds after a shape came into view and when it was close enough, Vex could tell it was a dolphin.

The dolphin took him on its back and swam up to the surface with Vex at an incredibly gentle and slow pace. When they reached the surface Vex's lungs were just about to pop. Vex was so exhausted, but he did look down at the dolphin to say thank you. As he did so, he realized that the dolphin was missing a fin.

"You saved my life, even though you are very hurt yourself. Thank you!"

Just when he had finished his sentence and genuine gestures of appreciation to the dolphin, the biggest creature he had ever seen with huge teeth torpedoed up from the dark ocean, snatched up the dolphin and swallowed it whole. Blood was draining down from the creature's mouth. The creature looked somewhat like a dragon but it had no wings and no arms. It had legs though, with massive claws on the end of every toe.

The scary creature looked directly at Vex. He returned the stare but his eye color had changed from the comforting brown to the bloody red. The creature screamed. It sounded like a half dog, half cat scream. Then the creature howled one more time and it jumped back into the darkness of the Pacific Ocean with a huge splash.

"Wauw, -that was a peculiar experience", Vex thought …"What on earth was that ?"

## CHAPTER 2
# RESCUED

Vex dug around in his pocket and he found his GPS and pressed the big red button which said SOS on top of it. Now Vex just had to wait until the government would send a specialist team in their big dark blue helicopter for his rescue.

An hour later Vex heard a relieving rumble. He looked up at the pale, blue sky and saw a beast of a helicopter, striding across the sky. Vex pressed the red button again and now he could hear a loudspeaker being calling for him.

Vex smiled silently and with some satisfaction of the day's achievement. He had prevented Charlie and Thiago Fernando Rodriguez from poisoning the sea with the tear of the ancient Chinese dragon, he had killed Charlie, one of the world's gruesome bandits, he had survived the Japanese engine, the fourth most powerful bomb in the world, with the great assistance from a dolphin he was prevented from drowning, he had chased a huge and remarkably strange sea creature off and finally in awaiting his rescue at sea, he hadn't frozen to his death in the cold and unforgiven water. All in all, this day's mission was a success.

A ladder was pulled down for Vex to climb up. Vex hesitated and then took a hold on the ladder, all his muscles screaming with exhaustion and pain as he hauled himself up the ladder. When he was at the top his wife Mary and his small baby son were there as well in the helicopter to help rescuing him. Vex gave them kisses and a big hug and then he just dumped to the floor with an overwhelming fatigue.

## CHAPTER 3
# THE EVIL MASTER-MIND

"I hear that you failed the mission and that Charlie is dead" The man said. His massive bodyguard was standing looming over them all.

"This is true, but at least I killed Vex with the Japanese Engine, so now we don't have to worry about him, his family and his constant interference in our affairs" Thiago Fernando Rodriguez said.

"I told you I wanted the girl!" The man snapped back.

"Calm down Mr. Crox" Thiago tried.

"No! I want the girl. That is to be your next mission! When you return with her, then you may make another sea trip, this time out into the Atlantic Ocean!" The man called Mr. Crox growled.

Thiago, to Mr. Crox's surprise, smiled in a reassuring and confident way. Thiago of course smiled because he was about to find and capture the most beautiful girl on earth.

"You get it?"

"Of course!" …and that smile again.

"But remember" Crox paused, clapped his hands two times and poked unquestionably Thiago's breast with a pointy finger, "the girl is MINE!"

## CHAPTER 4
# ON RECRUIT SEARCH

Thiago Fernando Rodriguez was in Spain looking for a new recruit to his terror organization. He was walking down a little street as a tall man with long black hair and a very pretty girl at his side passed them.

"Oh," Thiago muttered. "Hell."

And suddenly Vex was behind him. Vex wrapped an arm around Thiago's throat. Vex dragged him into a corner. Thiago struggled but it was of no use, the tall, strong Vex was better than him at all sorts of physical combat and martial arts. Suddenly, Thiago thought of something.

"You have the same power as me?" He whimpered

"Yes I do, but I have three questions for you, why are you in Spain?"

"Because, I am looking for a new recruit"

"Okay, next question. Are you worried that I am going to kill you, right now?"

"Do I look worried?", Thiago confidently responded.

"No, but neither do you look intelligent, so I am going to give you the benefit of the doubt. And third question, how did you get Charlie along with that weird plan of yours?"

"I learned to hypnotize people"

"Seriously? Well you won't get your new recruit this time around, because now you are going straight to jail"

Thiago's eyes were not focusing on Vex anymore though, but on the beautiful Mary and there was something different in her eyes. Mary pushed Thiago away and sent a knee into Vex's side. Vex stumbled but Mary came at him again with an elbow to his face followed by six other blows. Vex crumbled to the ground, helpless against the unexpected attack. The hypnotized Mary was helping Thiago to his feet and then they vanished, together.

## CHAPTER 5
# THE NEW RECRUIT

Thiago Fernando Rodriguez had never seen Neferin Crox smile so broadly when Thiago returned and delivered as promised.

"I have the girl, who is now also my new recruit. When my next mission is done, she will be your girl. This will be the deal Mr. Crox, -take it or leave it"

"Perfect!" Crox responded in awe of this surprising situation. He frowned for a moment "Why is she not screaming or anything like that?"

"She is hypnotized. I hypnotized her. She is completely in my control"

"You can hypnotize people?"

"Yeah, I hypnotized Charlie as well. In general I often hypnotize people into becoming the tools, that I need to accomplish my missions"

Mr. Crox's wet eyes that looked like colored milk had grown so big and so pale that Thiago thought for a few seconds they looked like fish eyes that were going to pop out of his head. All of a sudden, a boot came hammering into Mr. Crox's knee and he screeched as Mary hit him again. Thiago stepped in and slapped Mary across the face. "Do not hurt Mr. Crox! He is the boss! And if you hurt the boss he is going to simply melt your face. You get it Little Miss?!"

Mary nodded respectfully in her hypnotized state of mind, "yes, master".

## CHAPTER 6
# AT THE HOSPITAL

Vex opened his eyes and found himself at the hospital in a medical bed. He stood up, grunted, looked down at his bandaged ribs. Two broken and a third one fractured. Mary and Thiago surely had him roughed up.

"Are you okay sir?" A nurse asked as she hurried into the room.

"I'm grand." He replied

"We would like you to stay for some hours so that we can finish your tests. Is that quite alright with you sir?"

"That would be fine." Vex lied. Inside he was technically screaming and cursing, wanting to kill that crazy and yet incredibly smart assassin and terrorist, Thiago Fernando Rodriguez.

"I'm sure it will be over quickly."

"If you could hurry a little then I could probably even catch my flight to Italy"

"That would be possible sir. When do you have to board your plane?"

"In three hours."

"Very well sir. We can be finished with tests and scanning of your ribs in one hour."

"Great! Thanks!"

## CHAPTER 7
# LOOKING FOR MARY

Vex had searched everywhere for Mary, but she was nowhere to be found in her home quarters or in her usual environment. He had almost given up by the time it was diner when he suddenly remembered about Jonathan Johnson and Thiago Fernando Rodriguez being really close friends before Jonathan died.

Jonathan had lived very close to Mary's neighborhood. So Vex decided to check on the Johnson residence. Jonathan Johnson had lived there with his two brothers whom Vex also eliminated two years earlier. The Johnsons had been a real crime family in their golden days, but Vex had put a full stop to that adventure.

Vex arrived at the mansion and looked inside one of the giant crystal windows. To his surprise he spotted a man with frizzy hair and a tattoo of a fiery flame on his neck. Vex crept around the back of the house and entered through the cellar, gun in hand, he walked as smooth as a tiger and soundless as a ninja. He found an exit up some stairs and opened it.

Vex was greeted by a massive fist which struck him on the chin. Vex flew back down the stairs and landed heavily on his back like a sack of potatoes. He looked up and saw a monster of a man his muscles popping out everywhere and a fierce piercing in his lower lip. Vex's eyes started getting red but Thiago must have warned them that Vex had powers, so the man charged quickly at Vex while pulling out a tanto knife from his belt. The ninja blade looked sharper than a razor and it was only luck that Vex ducked under the swipe. The tanto knife cutting straight through the furniture where Vex had just been hiding.

Vex made a run for the stairs but he was punched hard in the gut by the huge man. Vex cried out. The man really had it in for Vex when he swung the tanto knife straight at his heart… Vex rolled out of the tanto's reach in the last second and jumped to his feet and took out his gun. He pointed it point black in the man's face. The man put up his enormous hands and then spat Vex in the face. Vex lost his sight and tumbled around blindly. He soon after cried out in pain as the tanto slit across his left arm. He felt the warm blood swarm across his arm. Vex started to feel a bit helpless, he had no chance against this monster of a Korean man. Vex wiped his eyes and then all vision returned to him. Vex then made one final, desperate move to beat the Korean. He clenched his fists and used his magic to transform them into large stone boulders. He then made a move that the Korean didn't see coming and soon after a single crushing blow from Vex, the Korean giant lay unconscious, slumped on the floor.

Vex knew that the fight had made a lot of noise so he was prepared for anything when he had climbed the stairs and opened the door.

## CHAPTER 8
# NEFERIN CROX

Vex opened the door a second time, hoping no more giants would be there to meet him. He was in luck, no one was there.
He crept inside and found himself standing in the middle of what seemed to be the kitchen. He sneaked out the door and saw Thiago, his back turned to him. Vex knew that this was a major chance for him in capturing his enemy, but before he could make another move, white hot pain flared through him and paralyzed his ability to move. Apparently, the tanto knife had been poisoned and since Vex had been cut during the fight with the Korean, the painful poisoning was taking over the control of Vex's body. He collapsed on the floor for the third time today (not one of his finest achievements).

The light suddenly appeared as Vex returned to consciousness. He was sitting in a chair tied with rope and tape. His wound, still infected from the poison and was hurting like hell. In front of him stood the mysterious man that Vex had seen through the window earlier. The giant Korean who appeared to be his bodyguard, had come to his feet again after

Vex's punch and now he stood behind him, towering over his boss. Furthermore, the people next to him were Thiago, and to Vex's surprise Mary as well.

"Thiago," said the man with the flaming tattoo. "Do your thing!"

Thiago stepped forward and looked at Vex, his eyes ready to hypnotize and fiercely trying to lock in with Vex's eyes. Vex felt that his self was changing, his urge to be on the opponents side was starting to engage. Like when you feel about to fall into a sleeping mode, Vex could feel the hostile hypnotization creeping in on him. Vex had to fight against it not to drift away from the person he really was. "Don't fight it Vex" Thiago said, "you may as well just surrender to my powers".

Vex then had an idea, he pretended to be hypnotized and then he would find out more valuable information. He had always learned that knowing the details of your enemy will turn out to be an advantage in a final showdown. Vex played the role and relaxed. Then he heard Thiago say "There you go, he is now fully hypnotized. –Sometimes I even amaze myself"

Vex was released from the chair and then Thiago told him all he needed to know. "We call ourselves The

Sorcerers, because we all have magic powers, except for the woman over there." Thiago nodded in Mary's direction. "We are planning on creating large sea creatures by putting the tear of the Chinese dragon in the Atlantic Ocean and whatever fish swims into the tear turns into a giant sea monster. The man who is standing in front of you is Mr. Neferin Crox, but we call him Mr. Crox. He is the ultimate boss okay?" Thiago was pointing at the mysterious man with the flame tattoo. "You know me of course, and the man on your left is Chi Lung." Thiago now pointed at the huge Korean guy. "And here is your beloved wife."

He signaled for Mary to step forward and Vex had almost snapped out of the act if he hadn't just been fed so much valuable information. He couldn't lose it all now by letting his temper get the better of him. Besides, Chi Lung was standing with that deadly, poisoned tanto knife of his, ready for another fight. Consequently, he concluded, that now was not the right and time to make a clever move. Too much at risk. So, he swallowed his anger and pride for now…

## CHAPTER 9
# PREPARING THE PLAN

Vex was escorted to his room by Chi Lung, who still gave Vex the creeps because of his size and strength. They opened a door and saw a room full of fancy paintings and a huge bed. "This is your room until we find a better place to stay." Chi Lung said. "We will leave for the yacht next Tuesday, okay?"
Vex confirmed the orders with a nod. This would give him three days to make an escape plan and get ready for revenge and even completion of his mission.

"We will see you at 8:15pm for dinner in the grand hall." And with that being said, the huge Korean left Vex and continued down the corridor.

Vex opened his bag and took out his pen. He then took off one of the paintings and turned it so that there was some canvas for him to draw and write on and then he began brainstorming his escape plan. But he would have to make sure that no one entered his room and discovered his scheme. If that was to happen, then they for sure would hang him or chop him into eight pieces or something ugly like that.

Therefore, whenever he left the room he would put the plan under his bed covers.

After Vex had paused writing and drawing his plan he put it under his covers and headed for diner. When he arrived in the grand hall, Thiago and Chi lung were there already. Vex found a chair at the left side of the huge dinner table and sat down. Soon after, Mary joined them, holding hands with Mr. Crox. Vex almost burst with hatred and anger, but luckily he stopped that from happening when he accidentally bit his tongue clumsily.

Diner was actually really good. There had been beef and turkey with mashed potatoes and brown mushroom sauce. For dessert there had been a delicious chocolate mousse with vanilla cream on top. They went back to their rooms at 9:45. The others went to sleep but Vex was still up through most of the night, planning and worrying about Mary. He was also anxiously thinking of his son who was being taken care of at his parent's house. Most of all he worried about his chances of him and Mary ever escaping and get back together as a family again. He stayed up for another few hours until he finally slumped into his bed at 4:00am.

## CHAPTER 10
# THE PLAN IS IN ACTION

Tuesday had finally come, and Vex was ready to put his plan into action. He was woken up by a loud knock on the door. He opened the door and to his dismay, he was greeted by Mr. Crox who stood there in the hallway holding hands with his beloved Mary. This guy really was a mad man. He knew very well that Mary was Vex's wife and yet he would show off like this in his face with a hypnotized Mary.

"So how did you sleep? You have to be dressed and ready for breakfast at 9:00 sharp." And with that he slammed the door in Vex's face. -Very rude indeed.

Vex was eating his normal breakfast, two apples, a banana and a bowl of cereal. "So how are we all doing today? Ready for the best plan in the history of plans to begin?" asked Mr. Crox.

You bet I am, Vex thought, letting a little smile appear on his face.

"Why are you so cocky, Mr. Vex?" Crox asked him, now he began to smile as well. Soon the whole table was laughing at the awkward situation, which only Vex knew was going to be his enemies' ultimate defeat.

"So where did you get your powers from, Vex?" Thiago asked. In his most pale and dull voice, Vex answered. "I experienced the great and powerful sensei fight. When he had won and beheaded his opponent he asked for a "little one" to come forward. He singled me out and whispered into my ear be strong young one, you can do so much more than you are aware of and when he finished, he simply vanished. I then knew that I had something unique inside me and since then, I have been practicing and perfecting my magic as well as my martial arts."

Vex finished his meal and then Crox said to everyone at the table that they should go to their rooms and get all their stuff packed that they needed for the trip. Then he disclosed to them that he would not be accompanying them on the trip because of his weakness against water.

"Everybody link hands with me." Thiago said. And when they did, they all vanished into the thin air. As if having been teleported through time and space, they were all now standing at a port Vex had never seen before and in front of them were a magnificent yacht. It was as white as a tooth and looked to be even more expensive than his house at home. On the side of the boat it said: The Sorcerer's Pet. They advanced to the boat and Mary was the first to onboard.

Vex smiled to himself, as he remembered the scientific facts about how salt water will erase and obsolete hypnotism. So, he would soon push Mary into the water and then give her a signal to just play with him on the act and ultimate plan to defeat the enemies.

After a good 30 minutes sailing Vex decided it was time to get Mary back to reality. He went out to the side of the boat where Mary was standing. He then gave her a gentle push and she let out a heap in surprise as she went overboard. Vex looked over the railing and saw Mary surface. "Play with me on the act" he said. She immediately understood the situation and nodded, looking a little dazed of what had just happened. Vex cried out "Man over board…. or rather Woman overboard!", then ran to the bridge and found Chi Lung who was sailing and told him to stop the boat as Mary had fallen off the boat. The boat was stopped and returned to find Mary in the waves. Vex helped her gently out of the water. She nodded a little thank you to Vex and then whispered that she would get Chi Lung's attention so that Vex could find Thiago and stop his miserable plan before it was too late. But what Vex and Mary didn't know was that it in fact, their scheme already was too late to be put into action.

## CHAPTER 11
# SCUBA DIVING

Vex found Thiago and asked him if he could see the Chinese dragon tear but to Vex's horror this is what Thiago responded: "I already threw it in?" A vicious smile appeared on his face. Compelled to now snapping out of the act, Vex grabbed the nearest harpoon and shot Thiago in the shoulder. "What the hell have you done?!" He shouted is complete surprise and obvious pain, his words hitting Vex like boulders. Again, he magically vanished. But it wasn't over yet, Vex had to get on the scuba gear and scuba dive down for the crystal black tear. He found a cup with a lid on and then he flung himself into the Atlantic Ocean.

Vex had been intensely searching for about 20 minutes before he spotted the tear, gleaming in the water while it was slowly descending. Having scuba dived at the Maldives at several occasions Vex knew the different ways to ascent, descent, under water emergency procedures and scuba stuff like that. Vex kicked with all his might, carefully not to lose consciousness because of the fast descent. Vex was tiring fast because of the pressure and oxygen change. He was now only 10 meters way from the pearl. With his last pieces of strength he battled his way further down until he was about a meter away from the tear. He got the cup with a lid out of his scuba pocket and slowly reached out with the glass, carefully not to touch the tear he trapped it inside the cup. He looked at his tank clock and management console and saw he only had five minutes left of oxygen. This is when that scuba course training comes in handy, he thought. However, he was now on very deep water, approximately 60 meters down. This could be quite critical, if he didn't manage the rest of his oxygen carefully for the ascent.

Vex was struggling to reach the surface without jeopardizing the crucial rules of ascent. The suit, belt and tank were weighing him down. So, for one last desperate move for survival, he took the suit off and exhaled. One last breath of oxygen was left in his tank. He then let go of the gear and started exhaling slowly while kicking for the surface. He had to make an "ahhhhhhhhh" sound while exhaling so that when he reached the surface the air wouldn't expand and his lungs wouldn't burst within him. He reached the surfaced unharmed, breathing heavily after the exhausting experience. He had managed to avoid decompression chamber. But at the end of the day, he was a very experienced diver. He grabbed the ladder to the boat and pulled himself up and onto the floor. He didn't get to know what happened next as he passed out when a club was smashed against his head.

## CHAPTER 12
# PIRATES

Vex opened his eyes just to find himself tied to a chair, again, next to Mary who appeared to still being unconscious. Vex didn't know where he was but for some reason he felt rocking, like he was still on a boat. "Nice job you idiot!" He looked behind and saw Chi Lung was also tied to a chair.

"First you make all of us think that you are hypnotized, then you trick me into stopping the boat, then you injure Thiago with a harpoon and after that we get attacked by pirates! You really should start getting a life!" He screeched. Vex ignored the big man's frustration and he tried to analyze the situation. This was the first he heard of a pirate attack.

Vex looked over in the corner of the room where he saw all their weapons and belongings. He wrenched at the roped but they wouldn't loosen. All of a sudden Vex had an idea. He would try to provoke and intimidate the Korean giant.

"Chi Lung, if you say I am an idiot then what are you? I mean you were technically the one who stopped the boat and the one who didn't win against the pirates."

Vex's simple trick of provocation had worked. The giant fumed with anger that he was able to loosen his ropes and escape. He charged at Vex, but Vex was ready for him. The second before Chi Lung reached him Vex stood up in his chair and ran backwards charging directly against Chi Lung.

The impact power was immense. The chair splintered into a million pieces, the giant slumped to the ground in an unconscious state. Vex had been thrown halfway across the room and landed hard on his left hand. Vex didn't think it was broken but he was still hurt. He stood up, brushing the dirt away, grimacing at the pain and then went to untie Mary from her chair. He then went over and got his gun. He also took the tanto knife and walked over to Chi Lung."Sorry, nothing personal, but you are simply too dangerous to have on my tail. It has to end." He bent down on his knees and blew out the giant's candle with the poisonous tanto.

Mary was awake a few minutes after. They headed out the door and found themselves on a big ship full of dancing and drunk pirates. Vex and Mary quietly walked over to the yacht which was being dragged along with the pirate ship. They went onto it only to be greeted by a very ugly man who looked to be in his 40s. He smiled, toothless with dark red gums. He took a revolver from his pocket and aimed at Mary. Vex threw himself, pushing Mary away while throwing the tanto at the man. It embedded itself in his forehead, blood oozing out of his mouth as he dropped to the floor, lifeless as a deflated dull. Vex and Mary climbed onto the boat. Suddenly they heard shouts coming from behind. They spun on their heels to see six pirates storming at them, with what looked to be shurikens, the star formed throwing blades, which can be deadly if handled correctly.

The pirates, looking as fearful as they are, threw three shurikens at a time. Clearly, they were not specialists in this sort of Asian weaponry. One of the pirates, a tall thin man, threw a shuriken weirdly and it embedded itself in a smaller, more round pirate's gut. The injured man crumbled to the ground immediately, clutching his gut. Vex knew they had to think fast. Mary knew how to sail a boat and Vex cut the chain that was keeping the yacht attached to the pirate ship and when he had done so, Mary started the engine and they raced away from the pirates. At that point Vex thought they had escaped all evil, but boy he was wrong. Suddenly, you could hear a swooshing sound as a silver shuriken hit its target dead center.

## CHAPTER 13
# ONE MAKES IT, ANOTHER DOESN'T

"NOOO!!!!!!!!" Vex cried out as the shuriken sliced into Mary's neck. He ran to her rescue but he was stopped when a second shuriken struck him in the leg. He cried out in pain and stumbled to the ground. Mary was on her back, spitting blood, pain shooting through her body. Vex had to do something quick or else Mary would not make it. But what happened next, Vex could do nothing about. The spooky sea creature appeared at the water's surface.

It then rose up until it was towering above the boat. It roared and was about to attack, but then luckily a shuriken flew past Vex's head and found its way into the creatures roaring mouth. The creature stopped roaring instantly. It looked around a bit, somewhat confused, and saw the man who had thrown the shuriken. The creature jumped into the water and disappeared, three seconds later it jumped up from the other side of the boat and snatched the man's head off clean. The headless body was swung over the railing at the same time. The sea creature did not come back. Vex's mouth was wide open with astonishment, he smiled. He turned and then all humor and high spirits left him as he saw Mary's lifeless body sprawled on the floor.

"AAAAHHHHHHH!!!" Vex shouted as he had just checked for a pulse and there wasn't any signs of life. Tears welled up inside him and that is when Vex became a ruthless, heartless killer. At least when concerned his enemies. And these pirates were clearly not friends. He took the shuriken from his leg and stood up, ignoring the pain. He looked over the railing to see another pirate in the water. "He must have fallen in because of the sea monster's attack" Vex mumbled to himself. Vex took aim and flung the shuriken. It was a difficult target in the waves.

The man screamed as the shuriken sliced his left hand off. Vex was slightly disappointed about his aim but then he remembered that blood attracts sharks. And sure enough, a few minutes later a giant shark that only could have been a great white snatched both of the man's legs in one bite. He screamed even louder, color draining from his face. Vex took the tanto that was embedded in the other pirates forehead, what a brutal death. Vex aimed another time, this time with the tanto which he was more comfortable with. He aimed, and then threw. The screams were shut down as the tanto disappeared into the man's chest. Vex ultimately showed some mercy and gave the pirate a relief from the merciless agony.

Vex picked up Mary's corpse and put it in the captain's room. He then took hold of the rear and put on the boat's motor and sailed home. But Vex was not done, he swore revenge and would hunt Thiago and Crox until they both bowed in the dust before him.

## CHAPTER 14
# NEW SKILL

Vex had been practicing for hours when he finally found a type of magic that was worthy enough for Neferine Crox's death. He also managed to find a great type of magic that would torture Thiago in an adequate way. Earlier that day he had bought two fake corpses from the magic science facility, for testing his magic. He put them in a standing position against the wall and began.

He figured that Crox would have new bodyguards in place already. So he imagined he had just beheaded one of the bodyguards and picked up his head, in this case he picked up a baseball, and with his new magic he flung the head (baseball) and it flew straight through the first corpse's head, leaving a hole through the forehead of the dead man. He then raised his hands and you could hear the intestines boiling and popping inside the second dead man's body. Vex was very happy about these new well trained skills that he planned to use in getting revenge for Mary's death.

## CHAPTER 15
# A GREAT BATTLE

Vex arrived at their magnificent mansion and to his disappointment, seven new bodyguards stood around Crox and the bandaged Thiago. Vex tip toed around the corner and opened the door. All heads turned around and were surprised to see the tall and powerful man standing in the doorway.

"Where is Mary?" Crox asked "And where the hell is Chi Lung?"

"I killed Chi Lung with his own poisoned blade." Vex had to fight back tears at the mention of what was coming next. "Mary is dead…and even though it wasn't by your hand directly, I hold you responsible for what happened to my wife. "

Crox screeched and then signaled to his bodyguards to kill Vex. But Vex was ready for them. He snapped his fingers and the first two bodyguards fell to the ground, choking on their own blood. He then made his fists into granite and penetrated the third bodyguard's chest, grabbing his heart and then wrenched it out of his body. The fourth was obviously also able to do some sort of magic. His hands turning to razor sharp swords. He sliced, Vex barely avoiding the strike but hit back with one of his own. The man flew through the room and out the window. The fifth bodyguard was a female, that came charging at him. Vex's eyes turned red and she screamed as she turned to black dust. The last two bodyguards fled but Vex took his knife and threw it. The long knife separating one of the bodyguard's head from his shoulders. The rolling head came to a stop at Vex's feet. He picked it up and threw it at Crox.

Crox deflected the head and it flew straight into the last bodyguard's back. Crox had never seen powers in action like Vex' display of pure force before. He stopped and fell to the ground with a permanent surprised expression showing on his apparently dead face. Vex turned to face Crox but when he did, Crox and Thiago had vanished, again. This was turning into a bad, bad habit.

## CHAPTER 16
# TIDES HAVE TURNED

"So where are we?" Neferin Crox asked after they had escaped from the house. He had clearly gotten a bunch of unprofessional bodyguards. But still, they were trained fighters and Vex had just killed them in a matter of seconds. For some reason this made Crox angry.

"We are in Wales, sir." Thiago answered.

"Why the heck are we in Wales? And why are we in this arena thing?"

"You will see."

"No, tell me why we are here?"

"To kill you." Thiago smiled. And moved towards Crox.

Crox looked up. "What?" But he did not get an answer, as he was punched in the face by Thiago. He staggered backwards, hands clutching his broken nose. He was punched again, this time in the gut. He went down. Thiago kneed him in the face and he blacked out.

He woke up, finding himself suspended in the arena, hanging five meters over a pool. He looked up and saw Thiago Fernando Rodriguez, a smirk on his face.

"What have you done!?" Crox screeched, "Am I not your boss? Am I not your employer, paying you handsomely for your services?"

"Now, now, Calm down Mr. Crox." He smiled. A man walked in behind Thiago, his left eye was missing.

"So," the strange man said, "the famous Neferin Crox. I was expecting something a bit more extraordinary, but then again, not everyone is perfect."

"I don't like your attitude. Who are you?"

The man smiled. "You do not need to know who I am, just the fact that I am the man who will put a definitive end to your miserable life. You may have noticed the Piranhas in the pool below you."

Crox looked down and was absolutely terrified at what he saw.

"Wait, I can help you." Crox pleaded.

"Sorry, the tides have turned." The man said, "and now you are completely expendable"

And then the rope that Crox was hanging in snapped, and he plummeted into the pool of hungry Piranhas.

## CHAPTER 17
# DESMOND

Desmond, Vex's father, was taking care of little James, Vex's and Mary's child while his wife was in the city at work. They hadn't heard from neither Vex nor Mary in weeks. They were starting to worry. What could have happened since Vex didn't answer his messages and calls? Was everything okay? The thought of James not knowing who his parents actually were, was tormenting Desmond. James would risk being an orphan. Alone, after Desmond and his wife passed away. It was important for Desmond to find out what had happened to James' parents, to his son Vex. He tried to call Vex one more time to see if he had any luck but still, no answer. He decided that some fresh air would do him good. He carried James in his arms and went to the local park. He put James in the baby swing and started pushing James.

After a few hours of listening to James laughing he decided it was time to go home. He walked out the park's gates. He walked across the bridge and heard a gunshot. He could feel the bullet barely missing his neck. He yelped and ran as fast as he could to the end of the bridge. Hope welled up inside him as he was getting close to the end. Suddenly white hot pain flared up inside him. He gasped and fell to his knees, clutching his shoulder where a knife now was sticking out.

"Run James." he gasped. James seemed to understand and wandered off towards the house. Suddenly more pain flared as someone kicked Desmond in the side. He looked up, a man who would have been handsome if it wasn't for the missing left eye. He looked awfully familiar.

"Where is Vex?" The man asked. His voice was deep and desperate. That is when Desmond remembered who his assailant was. His eyes widened with fear. How could this be?

"I don't know" he stuttered. This was the truth, but his assailant didn't care.

"Well, then you're are of no use to me, old man." He took a knife and stabbed it into Desmond's throat. Desmond spat blood and moaned. His last dying sight fell on his assassin. Those cruel, cruel things he'd done. And that's when Desmond's life left him, staring at Jonathan Johnson.

## CHAPTER 18
# JONATHAN JOHNSON

Ever since Jonathan Johnson had been "killed" by Vex, he had been hunting him down. Everyone had thought he was dead. The way he first had lost his eye to a hungry crow and then had been penetrated by a spear had really convinced everyone he was finished. He had even been buried alive. It had taken him all his strength to open the chest, which he lay in, but also getting out of the grave. When he finally had dug his way out of his grave, he basically looked like a tall, dirty, naked zombie. He had walked into a deserted pub and would have been arrested if he hadn't strangled the owner who was about to call the police because of his odd and suspicious behavior.

He had stolen the owner's clothes and credit card and had found a hotel which he stayed in until now, when he heard that Vex and his new wife had gotten a child. He had been trying to hunt Vex down ever since. And now, now he had murdered Vex's dad. That was just a warning. He had a somewhat perfect plan, he thought. When Vex would return he would see his father's corpse sprawled across the kitchen table. And that is when he would find the message with his name on it, carved into the forehead of Desmond with a vicious knife. And when Vex found out Jonathan would hiding in the corner of the kitchen and jump out with a chainsaw and little by little, he would slice him to pieces. Yes, not even Vex had a fighting chance this time around. He simply couldn't wait for the encounter his enemy and taste the sweet revenge.

It was about midafternoon when Jonathan came to a place he hadn't seen in a long, long time. He smashed the window and stepped into his house. However, to his surprise there was a swarm of blood and bodies. This was a slaughterhouse. Who were all these people? He listened and heard something in the basement. He strolled over to the basement door, gun in hand, and opened. A vicious looking dog came running up the stairs. In its eyes you could see that it had only one thing in mind, killing. Jonathan didn't know whose mad dog this was or why it was here. He fired, hitting the dog's shoulder but the bullet bounced right off. Jonathan cursed and sprinted into the kitchen. He wrenched open the drawers, looking for knifes, but nothing was there.

The dog came into the kitchen, teeth showing. They were full of blood. Jonathan jumped up onto the table and took a hold of a pan. The dog jumped up onto the table as well but stumbled and fell forward. Jonathan realized this would maybe be the only chance he would get, so he didn't hesitate. He slammed the pan with all his strength down onto the dog's head. The dog crumbled to the ground and growled, but Jonathan kept smashing. Soon the dog's skull cracked and its brain fell out. Jonathan looked down at the brain and stepped on it. A soft squish was heard.

He somehow enjoyed this brutal and savage behavior, whilst imagining how he would deal with Vex

"I'm coming Vex." he said with a determined and evil smile.

## CHAPTER 19
# OLD FRIEND

Vex was so sad. His wife had been lost to pirate's cruelty. He was on his way back from the house where he had just fought an epic battle. He walked into his parent's driveway and saw police cars all over. Vex sprinted to the front door and stepped in. His mother was on her knees, crying. Vex took a hold of her, embraced her and asked her what was going on.

"Have a look for yourself." She burst into tears. Vex carried her over to the couch and put her there. He walked into the kitchen and was horrified at what he saw. His dad was dead. Vex ran over to the table his dad was slumped across. He pushed the policemen away from the table and read the message, carved into his father's forehead. Jonathan Johnson. Vex was horrified. And in that moment of distraction he saw a figure moving at the other end of the kitchen.

He turned and saw him. Jonathan Johnson was sneaking up on the nearest policeman with something in his hand. He was uniformed like many of the other officers working the crime scene.

Consequently, no one had found his presence suspicious. Vex couldn't figure out what it was, that he was holding in his hand. Jonathan was close enough to the policeman now that he put the thing he had in his hand and placed in on the man's neck. There was a soft crack as the man's neck broke like a stick. Jonathan dragged the body into the bathroom with himself. No one noticing it except for Vex who was standing open mouthed in disbelief. How could this bastard have survived? He had even been buried.

A moment later, Jonathan appeared again. Vex acted oblivious to the whole thing as Jonathan made his way over to him. That terrifying thing in his hands again. Vex spun around, catching Jonathan by surprise. His fists already made in granite mode. He swung, catching Jonathan full in the chest. Jonathan flew across the room. Everyone's heads turning by the noisy commotion. The police took out their guns and pointed at Jonathan. But to everyone's surprise he walked straight at the nearest policeman and stabbed a knife into his throat. Everyone shocked at the sudden and deadly attack. Policemen cried as they let out fire. However, Jonathan avoiding all of the bullets with cat like grace. He cried out as Vex hit him again, sending him flying through the room once again. He stood up and shouted;

"Curse you Vex! Why the hell can you not let

someone kill you without having to make a huge racket? I tried breaking your neck. You would not have felt anything. You would just have died"

"This is my revenge after all those years of torture you put me through. I was an innocent man! You killed my parents, my wife and you drowned my daughter you heartless murderer. And I also hear that you killed my brother, heh? Well now you know what it feels like." He pointed at Desmond.

That is when Vex got a terrifying thought. "Where is James?" He asked, not daring to think of the cruel possibilities.

"Who?" Jonathan asked. Obviously not knowing about Vex' son, name or existence.

Relief flooded through Vex's body. PHEWWWWW!

"I don't know who you're talking about Vex, but still, I came here to kill you and I intend to do it. Sorry old friend." And that is when pain flared within Vex and he drifted out of consciousness.

## CHAPTER 20
# SAVED

Vex opened his eyes, Locked up in a godforsaken room again. Before him was Jonathan Johnson. Behind him were four other men. Vex saw that the third man had a bandaged shoulder and that is when he realized it was Thiago Fernando Rodriguez. What the hell was he doing here?

Vex was confused. This was a crowd of evil. He had been standing in a crowd of policemen. And still he had not been saved. How had this been possible? He looked behind him and that is when he saw the other six policemen in their own shackles, strapped to the wall.

"What do you want from me?" Vex asked. "You killed my father just so you could stun me? You, little, stupid and pathetic man."

"It is nice to see you too, Vex." Jonathan said, giving him a hideous grin, "-and in this miserable and helpless state, I might add"

"And Thiago, why are you here and where is Crox?" Vex asked.

"Oh don't worry about Crox anymore. I'm sure he has made great friends in the cage with the piranhas." Jonathan sniggered.

Vex was astounded by Jonathan's cruelty. Neferin Crox may have been a foul man, but no one deserved such a horrible death. Vex could imagine what was in line for him.

"And who are your other three friends over there?" Vex inquired.

"Oh, haven't I introduced you to them? Well, this is Jack Ronald." Jonathan pointed to a tall but very slender man with spiky hair and a vicious looking scar across his left ear and all the way down to his mouth. "Next, this is Loui Grenado." A huge man who looked like a wrestler, with tattoos across both his arms and a handsome yet deadly face. "My third man, I believe you've already met." Vex spit into Thiago's face. Thiago ducked just in time before the spat hit him but screamed at the sudden pain flaring through his shoulder. Even Jonathan started laughing at the pathetic attempt to avoid some spat. "And my last man, who is my personal favorite," the others grunted their disapproval but said nothing else "this is Ethan Castle." A handsome looking man, a bit shorter than Vex himself. He had piercing blue eyes and a tattoo of a dragon across his left upper arm. He looked strong but without the appearance of being overly good and experienced in combat. He looked at Vex, and gave him a hand sign. The secret hand sign that was used between people who worked together for England. Vex frowned.

"So that was my four men. You obviously don't need this information, now that you are going to leave this world within ..." He didn't get to say anymore because of the piercing scream of Jack Ronald. Everyone looked around at him and saw nothing alarming in the room. "What the hell is it?" Jonathan asked. No answer. Then suddenly the head of Jack fell off. Everyone stared in utter bewilderment at the headless body that fell to the ground. In the confusion a gun shot was heard and before anyone knew what was happening the great body of Grenado fell to his knees blood running out of the hole in his forehead where the bullet had hit him. The wrestler fell forward, dead as a stone. No one knew who was leading the attack, so Thiago took a hold of Jonathan and they vanished. That is when Ethan walked over to Vex. Vex thought it was over but then Ethan untied the ropes that were holding him and offered Vex his hand.

## CHAPTER 21
# LAST CHAPTER

"Who are you actually?" Vex asked, as they had escaped the room.

"I'm Ethan Castle. I was sent by the government to be your partner and also to tell you that your wife is alive."

"WHAT! Mary is ALIVE?" Vex asked, the happiness flooded through him as well as the doubt . "Where is she now?"

"She is in Spain looking after your son, in your house of course."

"How did they find out she was alive?"

"Well, they didn't. I did." Ethan said.

"Thank you so, so, so much, I owe you big time!"

"No problem." Ethan said, swelling with pride of having obviously helped Vex, who was his great idol.

"And you say that you are my new partner?"

"Yes. And I also thought that you might need someone by your side after such a downfall. You know, with your father and stuff."

"Well, thank you. But we can't stay here patching each other's shoulders. There is a gruesome and unpredictable terrorist out there. So Ethan, this is to be your first mission with me. Are you ready for it?"

"Yes, Sir!"

"Don´t call me that, -you have already saved my life once, -and even before we have kicked off our new mission."

"oh, okay."

"Well then let's start hunting down that lunatic!"

**DETECTIVE VEX**

**DETECTIVE VEX**

**DETECTIVE VEX**

**DETECTIVE VEX**

**DETECTIVE VEX**

Printed in Great Britain
by Amazon